The Greatest Picnic in the World

by Anna Grossnickle Hines

CLARION BOOKS · NEW YORK

For Lin, Steve, and Sue,
who began the Society of Children's Book Writers,
and for all the people since
who have helped it become what it is.

The full-color art was prepared in watercolor and pencil.
The text type is 14pt. Palatino.

Clarion Books
a Houghton Mifflin Company imprint
215 Park Avenue South, New York, NY 10003
Text and illustrations © 1991 by Anna Grossnickle Hines

Printed in Singapore.

Library of Congress Cataloging-in-Publication Data
Hines, Anna Grossnickle.
The greatest picnic in the world / written and illustrated by Anna
Grossnickle Hines.
p.   cm.
Summary: Sudden rain almost spoils a wonderful picnic that Buddy
and his mother have prepared.
ISBN 0-395-55266-4
[1. Picnicking—Fiction. 2. Stories in rhyme.] I. Title.
PZ8.3.H556Gr 1991
[E]—dc20   90-40003
CIP
AC

TWP 10   9   8   7   6   5   4   3   2   1

We packed it up
and stacked it up,
the greatest picnic
in the world.
Turkey sandwiches,
mustard and cheese,
pickles and crackers,
if you please.

Cheesy nips,
chocolate chips,
celery sticks,
licorice whips,
raspberry drink,
and grape, I think.
Nope....

Spilled the grape
and had a purple
baby brother
till Mother washed him
in the sink.

We added napkins,
they were pink.
And plastic cups,
a tablecloth,
stuffed green olives
for my mother,
mushy peaches
for baby brother.
We packed our basket
to the top.
We didn't stop.

We put in apples,
we put in grapes
and hard-boiled eggs
and paper plates.
And then there was
just room enough
to stuff…

10

11

...the leftover pizza,
just one slice.
Nice!

Then…
I got a nice big box.
We put in the blanket
and Mother's hat,
a shovel and pail,
a big red truck,
a boat with a sail.
But while I went
for my ball and bat
and superspiffy
baseball cap…

…my brother threw out
my mother's hat,
the truck,
the pail,
the boat with a sail.
So I put my brother
in the box
to keep him out
from underfoot.
"Now you stay put!"
But Mother said,
"He might tip
and bump his head."

So I trapped him
in a cage instead.
Mother got
the badminton rackets
and all of our jackets,
just in case.
We packed spare shoes
and extra socks,
baby brother's bear that talks,
tissues,
diapers,
baby wipers.

Checkers, cards,
three storybooks,
a fishing pole,
some bait and hooks,
insect repellent,
sunscreen lotion,
dark glasses and visors—
we'll be by the ocean.
I put in the Frisbee,
the kite, and some string.
"There," I said.
"That's everything."

Now into the car
with the picnic box
and also the basket.
Oops! Dropped the socks.

And last
we buckled
baby brother.
"Are we ready?" said Mother.
And I said, "Go!"

23

But no.
Mother could not find her keys.
"Buddy, can you help me please?"
So she looked high,
and I looked low
and found them behind
the radio.
"Okay now…
let's go!"

Oh no!
Plink.
Splink.
Sprinkle.
Pitter patter splat!
Down came the rain
and…

...that was that.

So. . . .

We had our picnic
in the hall. . . .
That's all!

JP
Hines, Anna Grossnickle.
The greatest picnic in the
world $13.95